D1386570

C333357345

To all the grandpas
and grandmas.

First published 2012 by Macmillan Children's Books
This edition published 2013 by Macmillan Children's Books
a division of Macmillan Publishers Limited
20 New Wharf Road, London N1 9RR
Basingstoke and Oxford
Associated companies throughout the world
www.panmacmillan.com

ISBN: 978-1-4472-0259-2

Text and illustrations copyright © Marta Altés 2012
Moral rights asserted.

All rights reserved. No part of this publication may be reproduced, stored in or introduced into a retrieval system, or transmitted, in any form, or by any means (electronic, mechanical, photocopying, recording or otherwise) without the prior written permission of the publisher. Any person who does any unauthorized act in relation to this publication may be liable to criminal prosecution and civil claims for damages.

1 3 5 7 9 8 6 4 2

A CIP catalogue record for this book is available
from the British Library.

Printed in China

marta altés

My Grandpa

MACMILLAN CHILDREN'S BOOKS

My grandpa is getting old . . .

Sometimes he feels alone.

But then I come along!

When he is with me, he smiles.

When I am with him, I can fly!

At times he behaves like an old man.

At times he's like a child.

Occasionally he doesn't recognise me . . .

but my hugs can solve it.

Some days,
I am his eyes . . .

Some days, he is mine.

Together we have travelled the world . . .

Although sometimes he gets lost.

My grandpa is getting old . . .

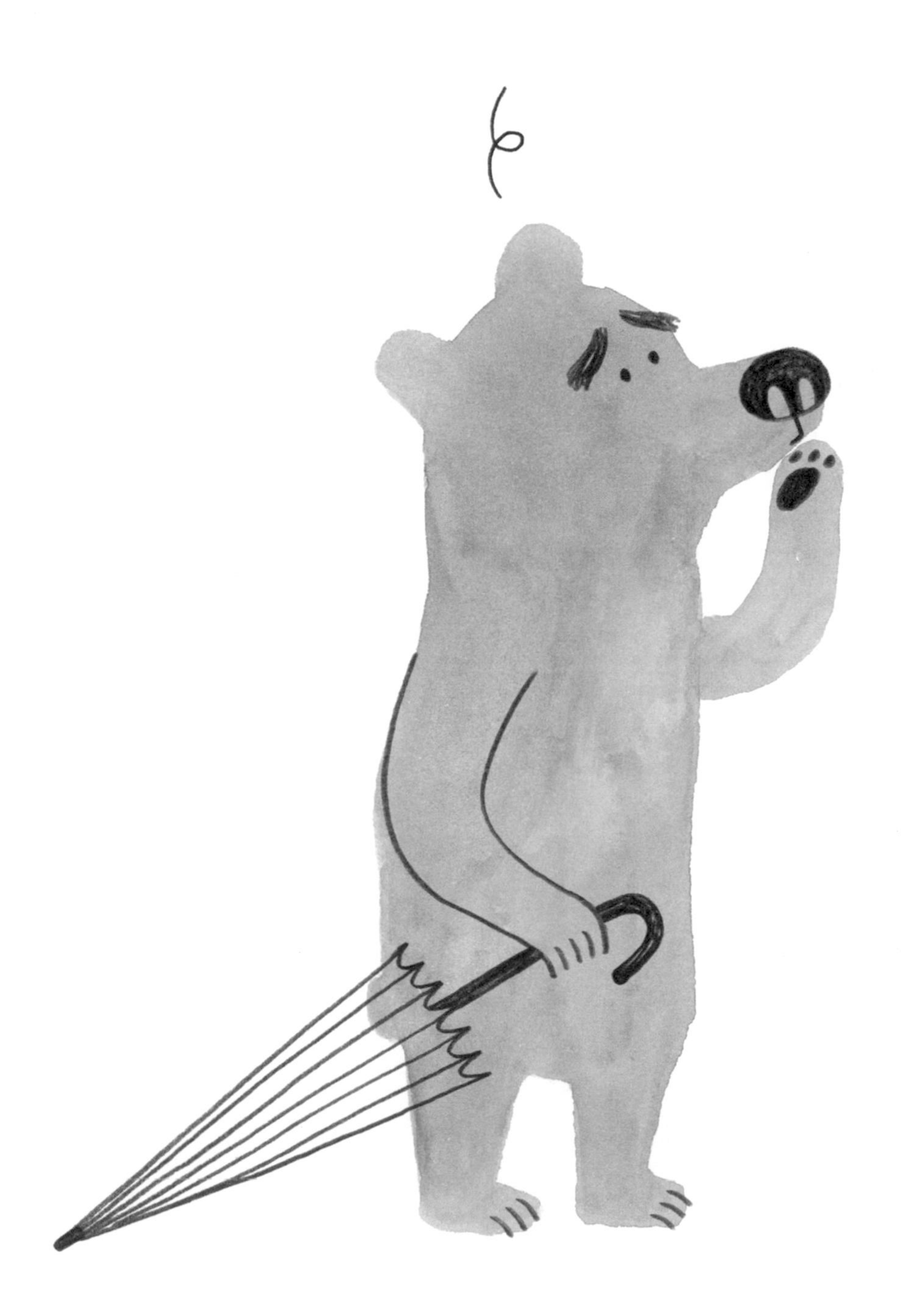

But that's how he is . . .

and that's why I love him.